Original Korean text by Jini Jeong
Illustrations by In Gahng
Original Korean edition © Yeowon Media Co. Ltd.

This English edition published by big & SMALL in 2015
by arrangement with Yeowon Media Co. Ltd.
English text edited by Joy Cowley
English edition © big & SMALL 2015

Distributed in the United States and Canada by
Lerner Publishing Group, Inc.
241 First Avenue North
Minneapolis, MN 55401 U.S.A.
www.lernerbooks.com

ISBN: 978-1-925186-38-3

Printed in the United States of America

1 – CG – 5/31/15

Crayon Road

Written by Jini Jeong Illustrated by In Gahng
Edited by Joy Cowley

The crayons make a straight road.
What will go on this road?

Cars and trucks will go on it.
Honk! Honk!

The crayons make a hilly road.
What will go on this road?

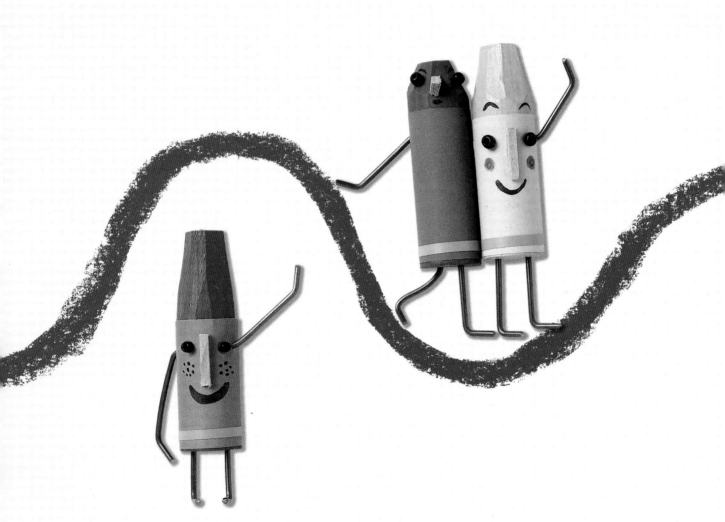

Bicycles will go on it.
Ting-a-ling! Ting-a-ling!

The crayons make a wavy line.
What will go on this wavy line?

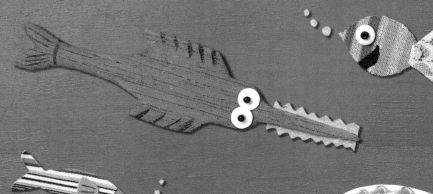

A ship will go on it.
Toot! Toot!

The crayons make
a long, long track.
What will go on this track?

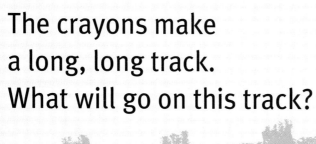

A train will go on it.
Puff! Puff! Puff!

The crayons make
a road with a bend.
What will go on this road?

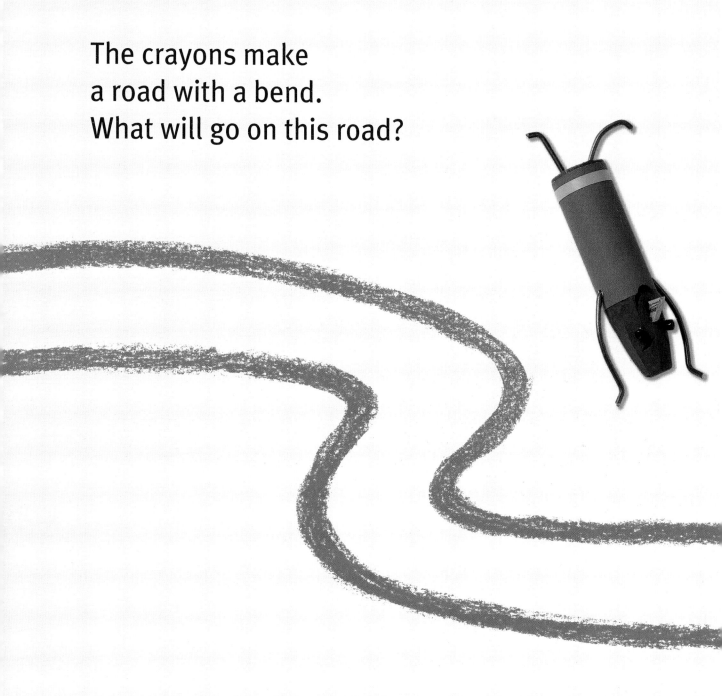

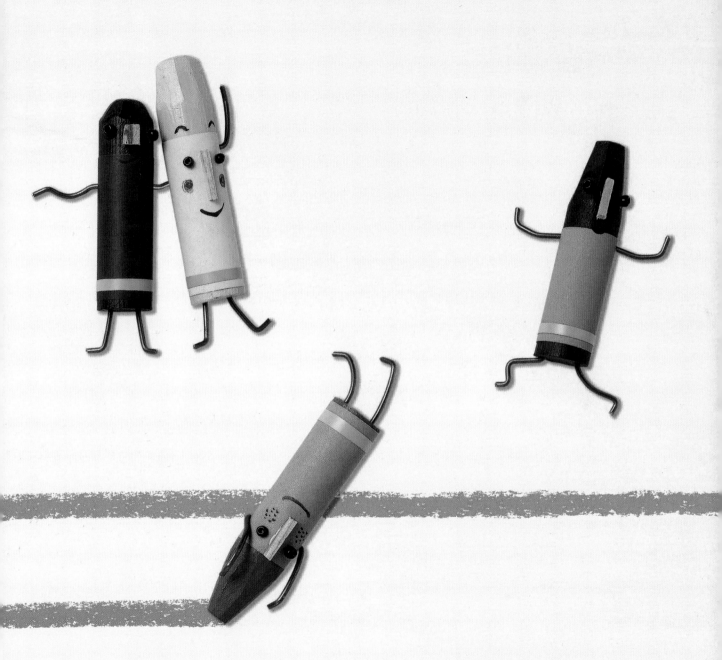

24

The crayons will go on this road to your house.
They want to play with you!

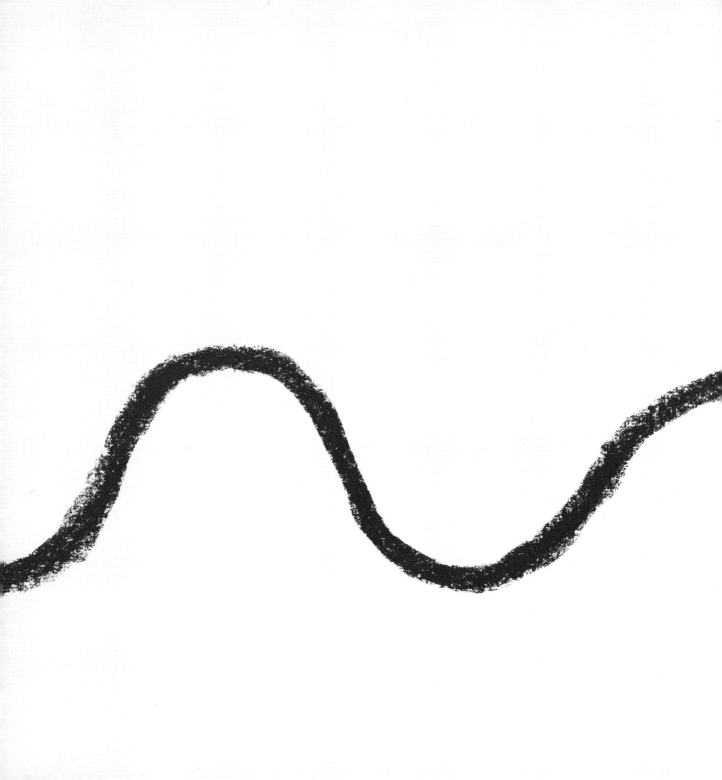

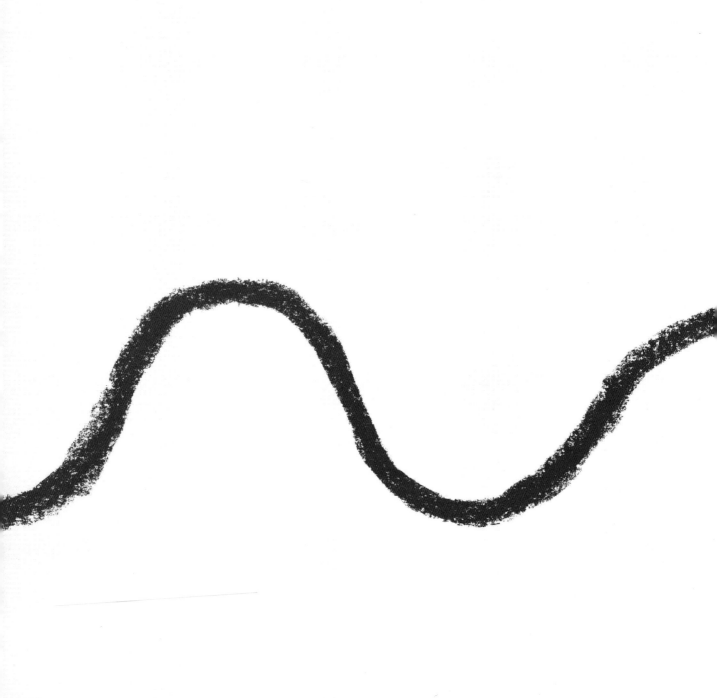

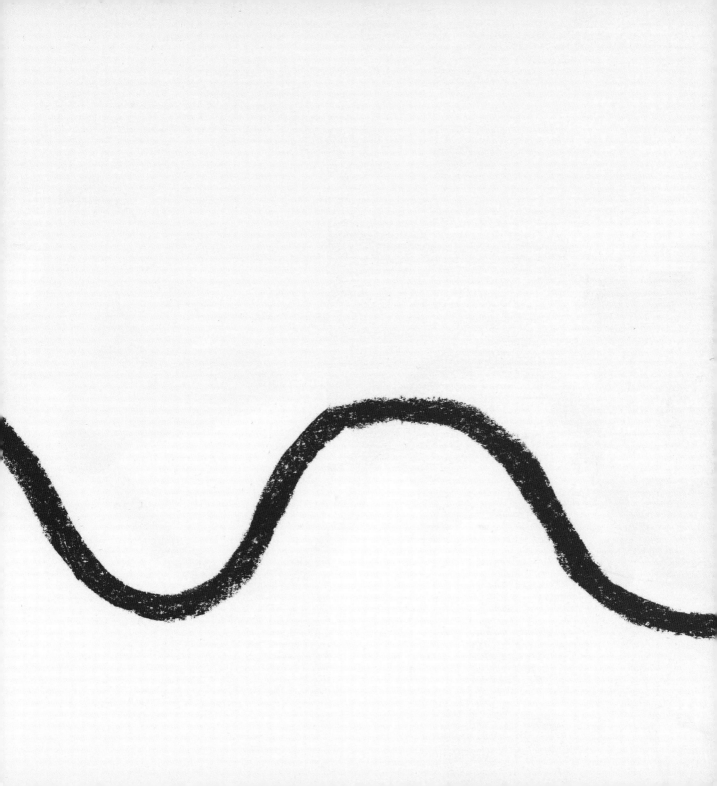

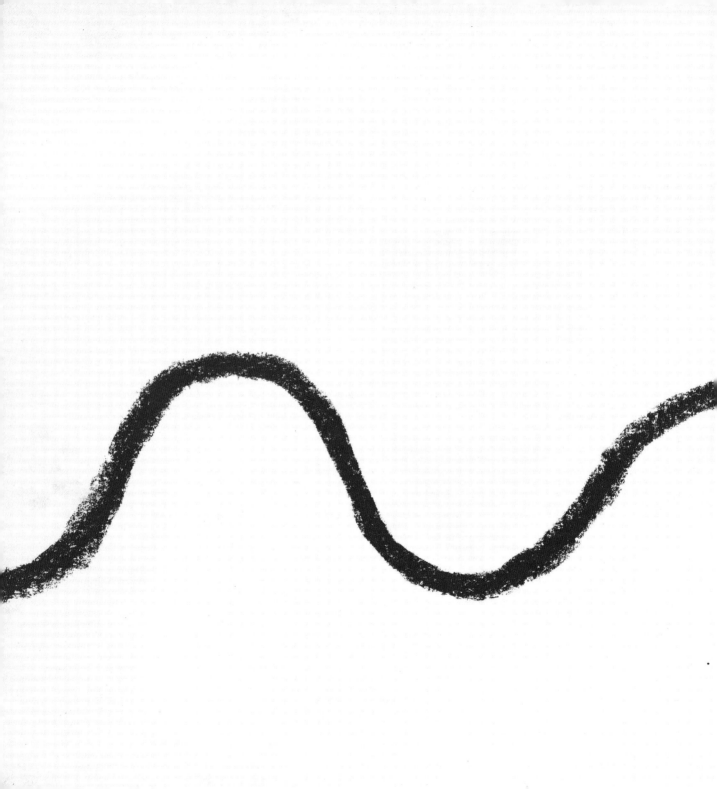